Theodora Bear

Carolyn Jones
illustrated by Barbara Spurll

ORCA BOOK PUBLISHERS

Library and Archives Canada Cataloguing in Publication

Jones, Carolyn, 1962-
Theodora Bear / written by Carolyn Jones ; illustrated by Barbara
Spurll.

(Orca echoes)

ISBN 978-1-55143-496-4

I. Spurll, Barbara II. Title. III. Series.

PS8619.O5325T44 2007 jC813'.6 C2006-907050-4

First published in the United States, 2007
Library of Congress Control Number: 2006940596

Summary: Harriet struggles to maintain order in a house filled with bossy
and demanding stuffed animals.

Orca Book Publishers gratefully acknowledges the support for its publishing programs
provided by the following agencies: the Government of Canada through the Book
Publishing Industry Development Program and the Canada Council for the Arts, and the
Province of British Columbia through the BC Arts Council
and the Book Publishing Tax Credit.

Typesetting by Christine Toller
Cover artwork and interior illustrations by Barbara Spurll
Author photo by Janet Rerecich

ORCA BOOK PUBLISHERS
PO Box 5626, STN. B
VICTORIA, BC CANADA
V8R 6S4

ORCA BOOK PUBLISHERS
PO Box 468
CUSTER, WA USA
98240-0468

www.orcabook.com
Printed and bound in Canada.
Printed on 100% PCW recycled paper.

10 09 08 07 • 4 3 2 1

This book is dedicated to Lenna Clara Harriet Erica Jones—the real Harriet.
C.J.

With love to my dad, whose quick wit, enthusiasm and creativity are deeply missed.
B.S.

Theodora Bear   Constance Bear   Brownie Bear

Vera   Ginny   Tiger

Lion   Snowball

Violet   Deborah   Eve   Frog

Lambie   Sheep   Annabelle

Chapter One
Sick Day

Theodora Bear was visiting Harriet. So far the visit had gone very well. The only problem was that there was no candy at Harriet's house. Theodora told herself that sugar was bad for her teeth and her tummy. And she had extra jam at breakfast.

Today, Harriet was sick. She was grumpy about it. She sat up in bed. She coughed and frowned in between coughs. Her animals crowded the bed. Theodora decided to cheer her up.

"Did you know that colds last ten days at most?" she said. "Only nine more days to go after today."

Harriet did not smile. She patted the bear and leaned back on her pillows.

"I once had a cold that lasted six weeks," Vera the penguin said.

"That's nothing," Violet the sheep said. "I once had a cold that lasted six months."

Harriet tried to speak, but the others were too loud.

"Only those of us from Antarctica really know about colds…," Vera said.

"Shut up, Vera. You don't get a cold from being cold. Everyone knows that."

"You do so get sick from being cold. It shocks your body."

"How shocking could it be if you were born there?"

"Well, I must say…"

"Quiet!" yelled Harriet. There was a silence.

"Some of you may have had colds in the past," Harriet said. "But I'm the one who's sick today. And I want some peace and quiet."

"Some people really like to feel sorry for themselves," Vera muttered.

"I agree," whispered Violet. "I don't think she wants to get better."

Chapter Two
Chores

Harriet was making her bed. It was the one household chore she really hated. She tossed Teddy and the others onto a chair.

"Why am I the only one who ever makes the bed?" she said.

Theodora looked up.

"Because you're the only one with thumbs," she said. "See?" She held out her paws. "Bears don't have thumbs. So it's hard for us to do jobs like that."

"Penguins don't have thumbs, either," Vera said. She held out one orange flipper for Harriet to see.

"Nor do sheep," Lambie said.

"Cats don't have thumbs, either," Tiger said. "But that's not why we don't make beds."

They all turned to look at Tiger.

"Well?" Constance the bear asked.

"We just don't feel like it," Tiger said. She curled herself up for a pre-breakfast nap.

Harriet finished making the bed. She put all the animals back, except Tiger. When Harriet left the room, Tiger jumped up on the bed. She pushed Violet off the pillow.

"Harriet's getting forgetful," she said sleepily. "And the blanket isn't folded back the way I like it, either. Could you wake me up when breakfast is ready?"

Chapter Three
Music, Music, Music

One morning, Harriet turned on the radio.

Theodora asked, "Could we listen to some different music today?"

"Sure," Harriet said. "Like what?"

"Do you have 'Teddy Bears' Picnic'?"

Harriet smiled. "I don't think so."

"Never mind, then," Theodora said.

Harriet hummed along to the music as she tidied her room.

Theodora said, "You know, you can buy 'Teddy Bears' Picnic' on a CD. It's quite cheap these days."

Vera frowned. "If you get that, you should get some penguin music too," she said.

"Like what, Vera?" Theodora asked. "'Baby, It's Cold Outside'?"

The others giggled.

"Or maybe 'Frosty, the Snowman'?" Theodora said. The laughter rose again.

"Stop!" Harriet shouted. "How can you be so mean to Vera? That's it! No special music for anyone!"

"Except you, Harriet," Theodora muttered.

"Do you have a problem with that?" Harriet asked.

"Oh, no! No-ho-ho," Theodora said. "Not at all, no-ta-tall. Noooo." And she began to hum 'Teddy Bears' Picnic.' She was a little off-key.

Chapter Four
Movie Night

Harriet liked to read books or listen to music at home. Sometimes her friend Carla talked her into watching a video.

"It's relaxing," Carla said.

"It used to be," Harriet said.

The girls pulled the two couches and the big chair into place. Then they began bringing out all the animals.

"I think it's my turn in the big chair," Lambie said. Harriet made room for Lambie.

"Excuse me," Constance said. "Could I have a cushion, please?"

Harriet went into the spare room. She brought out all the extra pillows. At last, all the animals were settled.

They had blankets, pillows, cushions, drinks and snacks. Theodora held the remote control. Harriet and Carla squeezed onto either end of a couch.

"Excuse me," Sheep said, crossly, to Harriet. "I can't see through your head!"

Harriet sighed and moved onto the floor.

Theodora pressed Play.

"It's not easy to use a remote with paws," she said.

The movie started. It was *Mary Poppins*. At first, everyone watched.

Then, "I wish they didn't have those funny accents," Theodora said. "I can't understand what they're saying."

"We do not call people's accents funny, Teddy," Harriet said. "It's not polite. Anyway, your accent would sound just as funny to people in England."

"I don't have an accent," Theodora said.

"Everyone has an accent, Theodora. You just don't notice yours because you're used to it," Harriet said.

"What kind of accent?" Theodora asked.

"What?" Harriet said.

"What kind of accent do I have?" Theodora asked.

"I can't explain now! I'm watching the movie!"

"I think we'd better rewind a little," Carla said.

They settled down again to watch. After a while, many of the younger animals fell asleep. Some of them snored.

At midnight the movie ended. Harriet said, "I don't understand why Mary Poppins had to leave."

"She said that she would stay until the wind changed," Carla said.

"When did she say that?" Harriet asked.

"When the kids first talked to her. Remember?"

Harriet shook her head. "I must have missed that bit."

"I have an idea," said Theodora as she was carried off to bed. "Why don't we watch the movie again tomorrow night? That way, you can figure it out better."

"No, thanks," Harriet said. "Tomorrow night I want to relax."

Chapter Five
Theodora Bear Goes Camping

Theodora Bear was, in general, easy to get along with. Only one thing bothered her: She got upset when people were mean about bears.

Harriet once made the mistake of saying, "I can't bear it when people are rude."

From then on, the other animals would say, "I can't BEAR it" whenever they wanted to tease Theodora.

Then Theodora got her revenge. One day she heard Harriet and Carla planning a camping trip. They were making a list. Carla said, "We always bring too much. We should stick to the bare essentials—just what we really need."

Theodora bounced away.

"We bears are going camping," she bragged to the others. "And you all have to stay home."

The three bears began getting ready. They tied knots. They found good hiking boots. They packed backpacks. In them they put water bottles, matches, string, fruit bars, dry socks and kazoos.

The night before the trip, Theodora gave Harriet the three backpacks.

"What are these?" Harriet asked.

"Just the bear essentials for the trip," Theodora said. "We got ready all by ourselves, Brownie and Connie and I."

"You're coming camping?"

"Of course!" said Theodora. "I heard you and Carla planning to take us. I know you were meaning to surprise us. The others are so jealous!"

Harriet thought for a minute. She smiled at Theodora. "Well, this is great," she said. "Now we're all ready." Then she called Carla.

The next morning, Carla and Harriet piled all their

camping gear in the hall. After breakfast, they came to collect the bears.

"I think you're so brave to come with us," Carla said. "You aren't afraid of roughing it."

"Roughing it?" Constance asked.

"Well, yes," Carla said. "It will probably rain half the time. There are sure to be mosquitoes. It gets very cold at night. And the noises you hear! It's different from the city, that's for sure. Are you all ready to go?"

Constance, Brownie and Theodora Bear looked at each other.

"Carla?" said Constance. "Did you say that it will rain?"

"It usually does," said Carla.

"Did you say there will be bugs?" Brownie asked.

"Sure to be," Carla said.

"And it's cold and scary at night?" Theodora asked.

"Pretty cold, yes," Carla said. "But the noises at night are mostly not anything scary, like a cougar. Just sometimes."

"I think I'm starting to get a cold," Brownie said. "It might be better if I stayed home."

"I think I'm allergic to bug bites," Constance said. "It might be better if I stayed home too."

"In that case, I think I'd better stay home too," Theodora said. "You'll need me to be in charge while you're gone."

"What a shame," Harriet said. "And you've got your packs all ready. Maybe you could play at camping while we're gone. We could set up a tent right here in the bedroom. You could all sleep in it. The bears will be in charge, since they know the most about camping. And we'll leave you a bag of marshmallows."

At this, the bears cheered up.

"We can hike out onto the balcony to check the weather," Brownie said. "And we can use a compass to figure out the wind direction."

"We can practice climbing on the furniture. And we can make different crafts every day," Constance said. "I want to learn how to make candles."

"We can sing campfire songs at night. And we'll toast marshmallows in the fireplace," Theodora said. "And we won't get cold and wet."

Harriet and Carla set up the tent.

Carla whispered, "Their way of camping sounds like more fun than ours."

"We've got two tents," Harriet whispered back. "We could set up ours on the balcony. We could camp right here."

That's how the camping trip became a home vacation. Theodora took all the credit.

After that, the others had to stop making bear jokes. Theodora would just say, "I guess you don't want to come camping next year?"

Harriet also had a talk with Theodora. So Theodora allowed the others to call marshmallows that were toasted just right "Brown Bears." They called burnt marshmallows "Black Bears."

Chapter Six
Christmas Planning

On March first ("Saint David's Day in Wales," Theodora said) the animals began making their Christmas list. Theodora had trouble using a pen with her paws. Vera helped by holding the paper down and giving advice. After a while, Snowball the cat came over and wrote the list:

- *one (1) small scarf, red or green, with a bear print*
- *one (1) bracelet, any style*
- *boots (2) (red or brown, with pictures of bears on them)*
- *candy canes (lots)*
- *chocolate (lots)*
- *marzipan (lots)*

Theodora gave the list to Harriet to mail to Santa.

"It's rather early, isn't it?" Harriet asked. "Santa might think you're a bit greedy."

"Santa likes people who are prepared," Theodora said. "After all, he gets ready early himself. He doesn't leave it all until Christmas Eve."

"But what if we think of something else we want later?" Tiger asked.

Theodora saw the sense of this. She said they would keep the list a little longer, just in case.

The list grew. And the items became more and more expensive.

Harriet began to wish that she had kept quiet.

In mid-April, Theodora told Harriet that their Christmas list was ready.

"Do you mean the list of presents you're getting other people?" Harriet said. "That is so nice of you."

"Don't you think it's a little early to start Christmas shopping?" Theodora asked.

"No indeed," said Harriet. "The more you do for other people, the more Santa will like it. And he's watching, you know. He wants to see if you're being naughty or nice."

Theodora looked at Ginny the penguin. They had had a big fight just that morning.

"Santa isn't watching us already, is he?" Theodora asked. "I thought he waited until later in the year."

"He watches you all year," Harriet said. Then she went out.

"That doesn't make any sense," Sheep said. "Santa should be making toys. How can he be making his naughty-and-nice list at the same time?"

"Maybe he sends out some of the work," Annabelle the elephant said.

"You mean to the elves?" Constance asked. "Aren't they sort of part of the family?"

"Well, we'd better make a list of presents for Harriet and Carla," Theodora said. "Oh, Ginny, here's that mirror you wanted to borrow this morning."

Ginny sniffed and took the hand mirror. She opened it, looked at herself, shut it and returned it.

"That's it?" Theodora asked.

"That's it."

They looked at each other.

"I'm sorry I was so mean when you wanted to use it," Theodora said in a low voice.

"Never mind," Ginny said. "I wasn't very nice, either. What should we get the girls?"

On Christmas morning, the animals got lots of presents. They were all books by Harriet and Carla's favorite authors. Harriet and Carla got lots of presents too. They got

• slippers with teddy bears on them;

• mittens with teddy bears;

• cell phone holders with teddy bears;

• mugs with teddy bears;

• a CD of songs about animals, including 'Teddy Bears' Picnic.'

Harriet and Carla felt very lucky.

Chapter Seven
Theodora and the Fish

Harriet, Carla and Theodora were out shopping. They were in Chinatown. Theodora was tucked into Harriet's backpack, looking out.

So far, Carla had bought a pencil case, oranges, tea and some buns.

Harriet had bought nothing. Harriet was a picky shopper.

Suddenly, Theodora yelled, "Stop!" She pulled out a paw and pointed to a tub of live fish.

"Do you want to watch the fish, Teddy?" asked Harriet.

"No," Theodora said. "I want to take one home. I want fresh fish for dinner. Which one is the biggest?"

Theodora stared at the tub. Harriet and Carla looked at each other.

"Theodora," Carla began, "I was going to get some of those dumplings you like. Do you want to help me pick them out?"

"No," Theodora said.

"Theodora," Harriet said, "how about some moon cakes? Those nice little cakes?"

"No," Theodora said, "if we take a fish home and then, you know, cook it, it will be perfect for my dinner. Fresh as fresh can be."

"Sorry," Harriet said. "We are not taking home a live fish. Do I look like a fish-killer?"

Twenty minutes later, Harriet and Carla were walking back to Harriet's house. Harriet carried a plastic bag filled with water. In the water was a large fish. Theodora sang a song, "Fish, fish, beautiful fish. It will make such a tasty dish."

When they got home, Carla ran water into the bathtub. Harriet put the bag into the water and opened it. The fish swam in slow circles around the tub.

Theodora sat on the toilet tank and watched.

"It looks yummy," she said.

"All right, Theodora," said Harriet. "Let us know when you've killed it. Then Carla will help you slice it up for your dinner."

"Me?" asked Theodora. "You want me to kill the fish?"

"Of course," said Harriet. "I'm a vegetarian. I don't eat fish. I certainly couldn't kill one."

Harriet and Carla left the room.

Out in the hall, Carla said, "That fish is as big as Theodora. She's never going to be able to kill it."

"Never mind," Harriet said. "We'll take it back to the store later. I just want to teach Theodora a lesson."

Back in the bathroom, Theodora walked along the rim of the bathtub.

"Here, fishy, fishy," she called out. The fish swam closer. Theodora blinked.

"Come here, little fish!"

The fish came closer still. Theodora stretched out her paws. The fish jumped into the air and splashed back under. Theodora jumped.

"Hey, fish," she said. "Are you putting on a show for me?"

The fish gave another leap. This time it flipped over backward. Theodora looked hard at the fish.

A few minutes later, Theodora came into Harriet's room. Harriet and Carla had newspapers spread out on the floor. They were finger painting.

"You'd better clean all that up," Theodora said. "We have to go shopping again."

"What for?" asked Harriet.

"A fish tank, some fish food, maybe some fish toys. You'll need a special light for the tank too."

"Sorry," Harriet said. "We are not keeping that fish. Do I look like a fish lover?"

Later that night, Theodora fed the fish in its new tank. She watched it swim around and snap up all the bits of food.

"What a wonderful pet," Theodora said. "She's quiet, she's clean, she's clever…She's like me that way, don't you think?"

"I think she's my pet, actually," Harriet muttered. "I'm the one who just spent a fortune at the pet shop."

"Mmm-hmm," said Theodora. "Say, Harriet? Don't you think my fish looks a little lonely? Maybe we should get another fish tomorrow."

Chapter Eight
Yoga

Harriet did not believe in watching television. "It rots the brain," she said.

She didn't believe in watching too many movies, either. "There are lots of good books to read," she said.

Sometimes, when Harriet was out, Theodora and the others would sneak out to the living room. Then they would turn on the TV and watch something.

One day, Vera thought they should watch the French channel. "We could practice our French," she said.

That same day, Theodora found a yoga tape. They watched that instead.

When Harriet got home, the animals were all over the

house. Each animal was in a different yoga position, except for Vera. She was studying French.

After that Theodora was happy as could be. She led the yoga class every day. She tried every pose. And it didn't hurt when she came tumbling down.

Harriet came home one day in a bad mood. Theodora told her to stand on her head. "It will calm you down," she said. "You do it like this." Theodora tipped over onto her head. Her back legs waved in the air. "It's very relaxing."

"What if you fall?" Harriet said.

Just then, Theodora did fall. Harriet fussed over her, but Theodora said she was fine.

"See? Nothing to it. You try it, Harriet."

"Maybe later."

Harriet went to the living room. She sat on the couch with a book and a plate of cheese and crackers. Before long all the animals had joined her. Everywhere, upside-down animals breathed loudly and fell with little yelps.

Harriet went to her room. She lay down on the bed to read. Half an hour later, all the animals were there.

"Shhh! Harriet's reading!" they said to each other over and over. They made a lot of noise trying to be quiet.

Harriet went back to the living room. She closed the bedroom door behind her. None of the animals could open doors, so she got to finish her book.

When she came back, everyone was on the dresser, right side up.

"What happened to the yoga?" Harriet asked.

"Oh, we're done with that," Theodora said. "We're all going to learn French, *n'est-ce pas?* That means *isn't it*, Harriet. After all, Canada is a bilingual country. How is your French, by the way? We could help you study."

Harriet ignored this.

"Am I going to have to listen to all of you practicing French all the time now?"

"That's right, I mean, *c'est ça,*" Theodora said.

"Well, what can I say," Harriet said. "*Je suis désolée.* I was just getting used to the yoga."

Chapter Nine
Counting

Harriet got bothered when the animals counted things. They counted how many turns someone got. They counted how many treats were given out. They seemed to count everything. The animals tried not to count, but sometimes things seemed unfair. Wasn't it right to point that out? Sometimes, though, counting didn't work. It didn't help them decide whose turn it was to sleep on the bed. Sometimes they argued about it all evening.

One day, Vera had an idea. They would make a plan on a chart. Harriet gave the animals some large sheets of paper. She gave them a ruler and a pencil. Then she left them to it.

"I think we should set it up in ABC order," said Annabelle.

"How about in the order we came into the family?" said Lion.

"Or by size, smallest to largest?" said Vera.

"Or largest to smallest," said Theodora.

They decided that ABC order would be best. Then they found out that some of the animals didn't know how to spell their names. Eve went out to the living room over and over to ask Harriet questions. After a while, Harriet came in and took over. First, she fixed some mistakes.

"Theodora, where does the letter *T* fall in the alphabet? Not right after *G*."

"Everyone's a critic," Theodora grumbled.

The plan worked well for a week. Then, one evening, Harriet fell asleep on the couch. She came to bed at two in the morning. Next morning, Frog said that she should get an extra turn. After all, Harriet had only been there for part of the night. In fact, since Harriet had woken her up at two o'clock, she should get two extra turns.

Harriet listened to the animals arguing for a while. Then she took the schedule down. She said she was going to decide who slept on the bed from then on. The animals were surprised.

"What made her do that?" Vera asked.

"It's hard to say," Theodora said. "I guess some people just don't like following a plan."

Chapter Ten
Names

"I think I'll change my name," Theodora said one day. "'Theodora' doesn't feel right anymore."

"What will your new name be?" Harriet asked.

"I'm not sure," Theodora said. "I want a name that shows my roots. I want it to make people think of the forest, and berry bushes and adventures."

"How about 'Rain'?" Harriet asked.

"'Rain'?"

"Yes, that's what it mostly does in our forests."

"Too plain," Theodora said.

"Okay then, how about 'Pinetree'? It's a kind of tree."

"Too boring. I want something sensitive, natural, yet strong…"

"How about 'Hurricane'?" Harriet said. "This morning you left your toys all over. The room looked like a hurricane had hit it."

Theodora gazed at her.

"I don't think you're listening to me, Harriet. Hurricanes aren't sensitive."

In the end, Theodora chose Theodora Bear, Queen of the Forest as her new name, Queenie for short. Harriet agreed to this. Lion didn't like it, though. She said that lions had always been the queens and kings of the forest.

Then all the other animals wanted new names. Name changes became the new fad. Day after day, talk about names went on and on and on. Harriet could not keep up with all the new names. And none of the animals would answer to their old names anymore.

"How else will you learn?" Theodora asked.

Vera became Teresa. A few days later she became Teri.

Theodora became T-Bear, Queen of the Forest.

Eve became Charlotte, then Charlie.

Constance Bear decided she would be known as Carmel.

Two weeks later, Theodora-Queenie-T-Bear and Lion-Brandy-Bree got into a spat. They both wanted the name Emma. They stopped speaking to each other. Harriet decided to take action.

"I'm changing my name," she told the animals.

Fifteen pairs of eyes fixed on her.

"You can't do that," Theodora-Queenie-T-Bear said.

"Why not?"

"We like you as Harriet," Theodora-Queenie-T-Bear said.

"*I* wouldn't change—just my name," Harriet said. "I was thinking Spider or Hungry Crocodile. Something kind of offbeat. What do you think?"

"Horrid names, both of them," said Theodora-Queenie-T-Bear.

"Not nice at all," said Vera-Teresa-Teri.

"Well," Harriet said, "I've been so nice about your name changes. I liked your old names better too, you know. And here you are being so mean about mine."

"Perhaps we could come to an agreement," Deborah-Elena-Ellie said.

After a long talk, they decided to go back to their old names. For months, though, Theodora and Lion fought over the title "Queen of the Forest." Vera finally talked them out of it.

"We're Canadians," Vera explained. "We don't need queens and kings. That was for back in the olden days."

"But we do have a queen," Theodora said.

"That's not our queen," Vera said. "She belongs to England. They just lend her out when we need a queen picture for our money and things like that."

Harriet opened her mouth to explain. Then she closed it again.

Theodora and Lion, though, agreed.

"Down with queens and kings!" Theodora said. "We're all equal here!"

After that the animals didn't use "Queen of the Forest"—except when they wanted to insult each other.

Chapter Eleven
Bedtime

Harriet had a big bed with two pillows and lots of blankets. It was bigger than one person really needed. But it was just right for a person with many animals. In fact, sometimes Harriet felt that her bed was much too small.

This evening, Theodora was leaning on a pillow in the middle of the bed. The other pillow was under her knees. A small blanket was tucked around her. The trouble began when Harriet wanted to go to bed. She said that she needed one of the pillows for herself.

That seemed fair. Theodora gave Harriet the pillow from under her knees. Then Harriet started to move her over.

"Harriet," Teddy said, "this is my spot."

"But you're right in the middle, Teddy," Harriet said. "Where am I going to sleep?"

"Can't you sleep on either side?" Theodora asked.

"Do I look like a snake? How do I do that? Cut myself in half?"

Theodora moved over a tiny bit. As soon as Harriet started to read, she heard a loud sniff. A tear was running down Theodora's face. Harriet dropped her book and hugged the bear.

"What's wrong? Are you sick? Did someone hurt your feelings?"

"You did," Theodora said, wiping her eyes with the back of a paw. "You didn't kiss me good night."

"Oh, Teddy, you're so silly. I'm not going to sleep yet, am I? Did you think I'd forgotten?"

Theodora nodded. "And after you'd been so mean about the pillow, and how much room I take up on the bed, well…"

Harriet kissed Theodora. Then she read to her until

she fell asleep. Theodora began to snore. Harriet woke up a few times in the night. Each time, Theodora was snoring loudly. And each time, Harriet was closer to the edge of the bed. Then she woke up to find she had no covers at all. Theodora had wrapped herself up in them in her sleep.

The next morning, Harriet went out early. She came back with the local newspaper. She began looking through the pages, yawning and rubbing her eyes.

"Has something important happened?" Theodora asked cheerfully.

"There are always important things in the paper," Harriet said. "But I'm checking out the sales. I think it's time to buy a bigger bed."

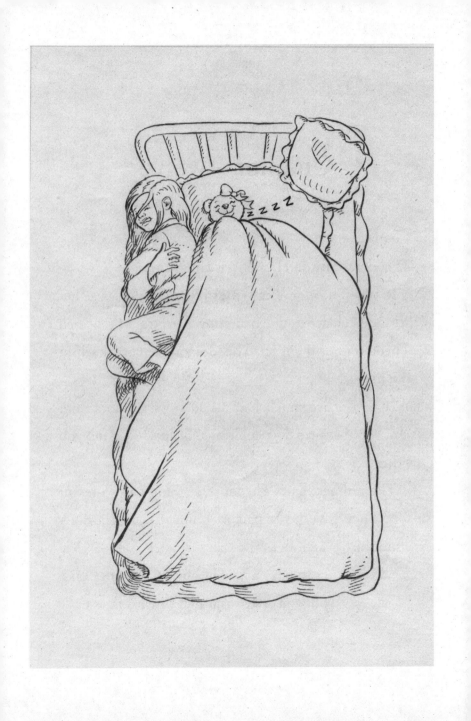

Chapter Twelve
Going Home

Theodora's visit to Harriet was almost over.

It was Theodora's last morning. Harriet gave her a blue necklace and a matching barrette. She helped Theodora put them on. Theodora looked at herself in the mirror.

"I don't have much hair, as such," Theodora said. "But the barrette does look nice in my fur, don't you think?"

The animals gave Theodora a going-away present too. They gave her a pair of binoculars and a book about bird-watching.

"It's so you can have a new hobby," Constance said. "That way, you won't have as much time to miss us."

Theodora loved her gifts. She went to a window and held the binoculars to her eyes. The bird book was open beside her.

"Look, there's a quetzal!" she called out.

"I don't think so," said Vera.

"You're not even looking!"

"They only live in Central America," Vera said. "They would have to be really lost to end up in Canada."

Then Carla came to get Theodora. Everyone said good-bye. Vera said *au revoir* to show off her French. Carla tucked Theodora under her arm and waved. Off they went, down the hall. Harriet and the animals could hear Theodora asking about lunch.

"I'm not sure what there is," Carla said. "We'll think of something. But I've got these great frozen éclairs for dessert. You'll love them."

Then Carla and Theodora were gone. Harriet shut the door and went into her room. She lay down on the bed and stared at the ceiling. She folded her hands behind her head and sighed. The animals had followed her.

They started to get worried. Soon they got up and left the room. Harriet didn't even notice.

Half an hour later, Constance, Vera and Violet came back in. They had one of the cookbooks from the kitchen with them.

"Harriet? Is it okay if we make burritos for lunch?" asked Vera.

"What?" Harriet sat up. "No, you may not. I'm not hungry. I'm too sad. And the last time you cooked, I had to spend the rest of the day cleaning up. And you almost started a fire. Remember?"

"Oh, that," Vera said. "Well, I'm sorry but we already started. We'll just put everything away again."

There was a cry from the kitchen.

"That's my tail, you wombat! Ow!" Tiger yowled.

Harriet leaped up and raced out to the kitchen.

"Put down that knife!" she shouted. "I'll chop the vegetables! Turn off those burners! We don't put sugar on burritos! Someone set the table!"

Vera, Constance and Violet grinned at each other.

"I don't like burritos," said Vera. "But they'll keep Harriet busy. She won't have time to be sad. Burritos for fifteen, coming right up!"

"We're only fourteen now," Violet said.

There was a pause.

"Well, we'll freeze one for Teddy," said Vera. "I'm sure she'll be visiting soon. We'll tell her it's a new kind of éclair."

Carolyn Jones has lived in New York City and Havana. She now lives in Vancouver, British Columbia. *Theodora Bear* is her first book.

Orca Echoes

The Paper Wagon
martha attema
Graham Ross, illustrator
978-1-55143-356-1

The Big Tree Gang
Jo Ellen Bogart
Dean Griffiths, illustrator
978-1-55143-345-5

Out and About with the Big Tree Gang
Jo Ellen & Jill Bogart
Dean Griffiths, illustrator
978-1-55143-603-6

Ghost Wolf
Karleen Bradford
Allan Cormack & Deborah Drew-Brook, illustrators
978-1-55143-341-7

Timberwolf Chase
Sigmund Brouwer
Dean Griffiths, illustrator
978-1-55143-548-0

Timberwolf Hunt
Sigmund Brouwer
Dean Griffiths, illustrator
978-1-55143-726-2

Timberwolf Revenge
Sigmund Brouwer
Dean Griffiths, illustrator
978-1-55143-544-2

Jeremy and the Enchanted Theater
Becky Citra
Jessica Milne, illustrator
978-1-55143-322-6

Jeremy and the Golden Fleece
Becky Citra
Jessica Milne, illustrator
978-1-55143-657-9

Jeremy in the Underworld
Becky Citra
Jessica Milne, illustrator
978-1-55143-466-7

Sam and Nate
PJ Sarah Collins
Katherine Jin, illustrator
978-1-55143-334-9

Sea Dog
Dayle Campbell Gaetz
Amy Meissner, illustrator
978-1-55143-406-3

Theodora Bear
Carolyn Jones
Barbara Spurll, illustrator
978-1-55143-496-4

Down the Chimney with Googol and Googolplex
Nelly Kazenbroot
978-1-55143-290-8

Orca Echoes

Visit www.orcabook.com for all our titles.